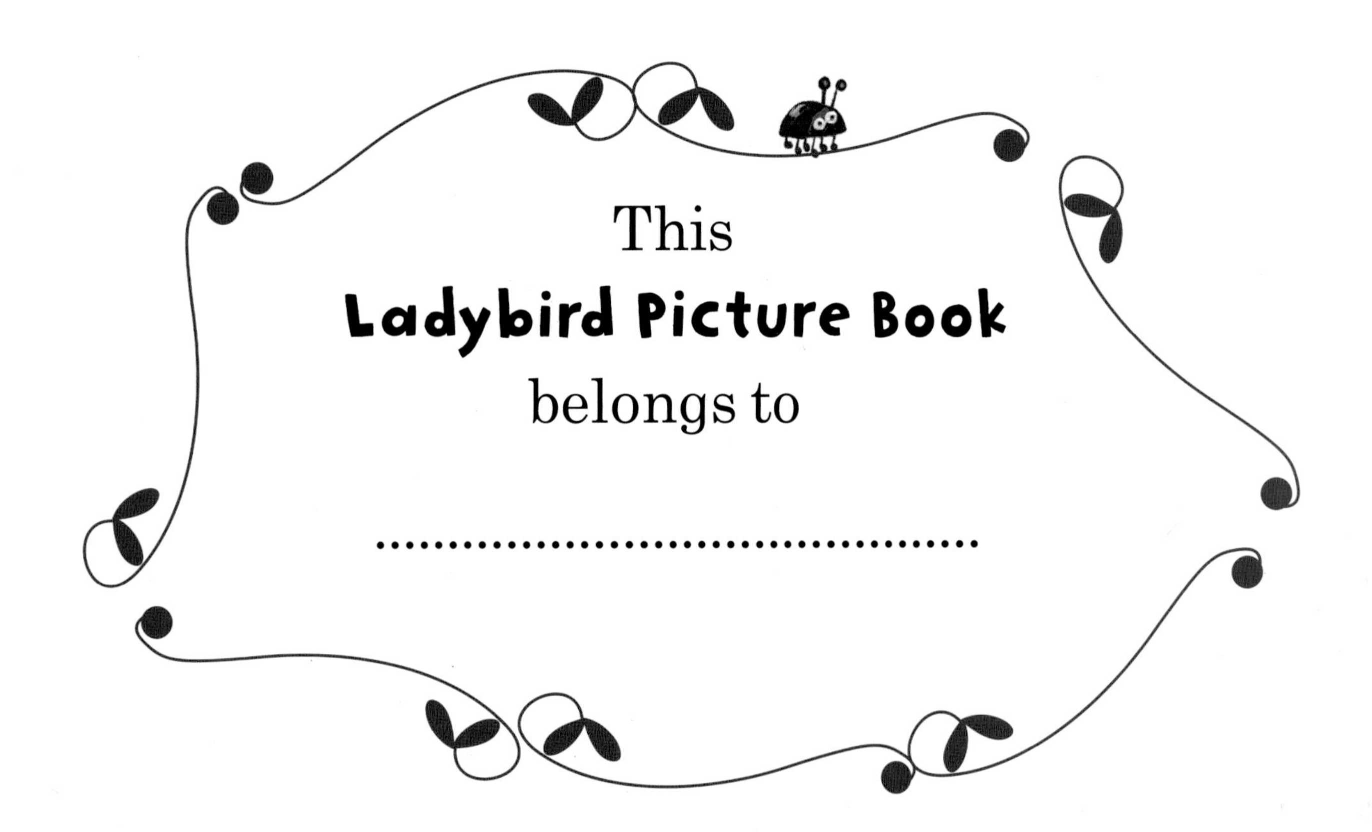

This

Ladybird Picture Book

belongs to

....

LADYBIRD BOOKS

UK | USA | Canada | Ireland | Australia
India | New Zealand | South Africa
Ladybird Books is part of the Penguin Random House group of companies
whose addresses can be found at global.penguinrandomhouse.com.

www.penguin.co.uk www.puffin.co.uk www.ladybird.co.uk

First published 1999
Reissued 2011 as part of the Ladybird First Favourite Tales series
This Ladybird Picture Books edition published 2019
001

Printed in China
A CIP catalogue record for this book is available from the British Library

ISBN: 978-0-241-38429-9

All correspondence to:
Ladybird Books, Penguin Random House Children's
80 Strand, London WC2R 0RL

Ladybird Picture Books

The Elves and the Shoemaker

BASED ON A TRADITIONAL FOLK TALE

retold by Ronne Randall ★ illustrated by Ailie Busby

Late one night a shoemaker sat
cutting his leather with a snip, snip, snap,
watched by his wife and watched by his cat.

"I'll sew the shoes tomorrow," the shoemaker said.
He went to bed hungry. There was no bread.
The cupboard was bare. Nothing there...

In the morning when he opened his eyes,
there on the bench was a big surprise.
Someone had stitched the shoes. But who?

The shoemaker blinked and scratched his head.
"What teeny, tiny stitches!" he said.
"Who could do a thing like that?"
"Not me," miaowed the cat.

He sold the shoes for a very good price, and bought more leather, and meat and rice. They had a good supper that night.

Then he cut the leather with a snip, snip, snap.
"I'm ever so tired," he said to the cat.
"I can't stop yawning.
I'll stitch these in the morning."

In the morning when he opened his eyes,
there on the bench was a bigger surprise.
Four pairs of shoes had been stitched in
the night!

The shoemaker blinked and scratched his head. "What teeny, tiny stitches!" he said. "Who could do a thing like that?"
"Not me," miaowed the cat.

Customers came to the shop in queues
when they heard about the beautiful shoes.
They tried them on...
Soon they were all gone!

And now with all the money he'd made, the shoemaker went to the market and paid for leather in blue and green and red.

He cut the leather with a snip, snip, snap, watched by his wife and watched by his cat. His wife said, “Now we’ll see what happens to that!”

Next morning when they got out of bed,
they found shoes in blue and green and red.
"Such teeny, tiny stitches!" the shoemaker said.

From far away, when they heard the news,
people came to the shop in queues.
“What beautiful shoes!” they cried.
“It’s hard to choose!”

The shoemaker sat and counted his money.
He thought, “Isn’t it funny! I’m suddenly rich,
and I haven’t even sewn a stitch!”

The shoemaker's wife said, "We have to find whoever it is who's being so kind. Let's watch in your workshop tonight."

So they left a candle burning bright
and there they hid in the dead of night.
Midnight chimed... the door went *creak*...

...and three little elves came skippy-skip in, with silver tools in a teeny, tiny tin, but their clothes were threadbare and thin.
Tip, tip, tap!

Their silver hammers went *tip, tip, tap,* and they cut and sewed with a *snip, snip, snap,* and the shoes were made in a flash.

When the elves had left, the shoemaker's
wife said, "I've never seen, in all my life,
three little elves, so threadbare–
I'll sew them all new clothes to wear!"

She sewed a tiny dress and tiny jackets
and tiny tartan trousers with pockets–
and the shoemaker made tiny, beautiful boots.

The very next night, they left the clothes there on the bench in three neat rows. Then they hid themselves to watch for the elves.

When the elves found the suits and the tiny boots, they put them on and danced through the door singing, "Shoes we'll make here no more!"

The shoemaker and his wife have never seen another elf.
The shoemaker stitches his shoes himself.
But every day he's grateful for the dinner on his table.

And every night to the window he creeps
(for he made a promise that still he keeps).
“Thank you, elves,” he whispers...
and then he sleeps.